THE SAND DOLLAR CLUB

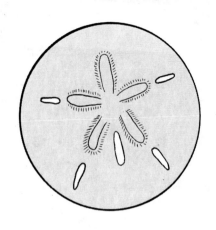
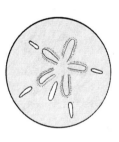
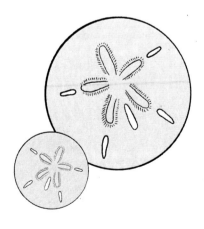

THE SAND DOLLAR CLUB

Ms. Sarah's Surprise

TATE PUBLISHING
& Enterprises

written by Annetta LaBarr

Published by Tate Publishing & Enterprises, LLC
127 E. Trade Center Terrace | Mustang, Oklahoma 73064 USA
1.888.361.9473 | www.tatepublishing.com

Tate Publishing is committed to excellence in the publishing industry. The company reflects the philosophy established by the founders, based on Psalm 68:11,
"The Lord gave the word and great was the company of those who published it."

Book design copyright © 2009 by Tate Publishing, LLC. All rights reserved.
Cover and interior design by Eddie Russell
Illustration by Katie Brooks

Published in the United States of America

ISBN: 978-1-60799-475-6
1. Juvenile Fiction: Nature & the Natural World: Environment
2. Juvenile Fiction: Religious: Christian: Values & Virtues
09.08.25

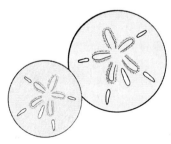

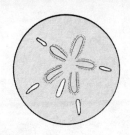

This book is affectionately
dedicated to my girls

(Wendy, Ariana, Marisa, and Sofia)

and boys

(Wade and Carlos)

who enjoy collecting shells at the beach.

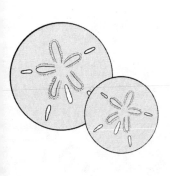

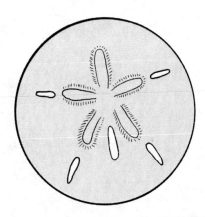

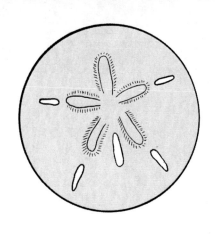
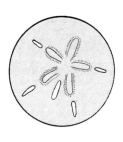
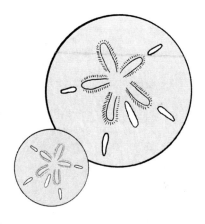

table of contents

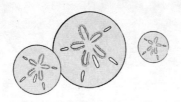

BACK AT THE BEACH

Paul created a lot of noise as he tried to get his suitcase, diving mask, fins, snorkel, and camera through the door of his grandfather's beach house.

"Hold on young man," his grandfather said with a chuckle. "You can't be in that big of a hurry to visit us."

"But I am," said Paul. "I want to unpack my things and go see if my

friends, Ariana, Marisa, and Samir are here yet. I only see them when I visit you for two weeks in the summer, but we do keep in touch with e-mails and postcards during the rest of the year."

Paul continued until he had managed to squeeze everything through the door and down the hall to his room. He wanted to find his flashlight, fishing rod, and tackle since he would need his fishing gear when Samir arrived.

Grandfather followed Paul and gave him a big hug as he said, "Right now we have time for a nice lunch since I know that Samir and Ariana arrive later today. Unfortunately, Marisa won't be visiting because her mom is having a baby and needs her at home. Come with me to the kitchen and I'll fry some fresh grouper for lunch. After lunch, you might want to visit Ms. Sarah at the end of the lane since she hasn't been feeling well lately; she asks about you every time I see her."

Grandfather and Paul walked down the hall to the kitchen, located in the back of the house.

Paul said, "This is my favorite room in the whole house!"

Grandfather quickly asked Paul, "Why is this your favorite room, young man? I thought you enjoyed my den with all of the books."

Paul replied, "Every morning we can hear a serenade of fishing boat horns as the boats pass each other heading out to sea. It is even better when you open the sliding glass doors and we can really smell the sea air."

Grandfather smiled. "You know Paul, I forgot that you don't live near the sea and only hear the boat horns and smell the sea air when you visit."

Paul sat down at the kitchen table while Grandfather started to cook the fish and make the hush puppy batter. The sun was shining brightly through the sliding glass doors and the light reflecting off of Paul's red hair made it glow. Grandfather suddenly realized Paul must have had a growth spurt over the past year because he was now quite tall for an eleven year old!

"Is there anything I can do to help you prepare lunch?" Paul asked.

"That would be very helpful, and

since you are always hungry we will eat a lot quicker if you make the salad," answered Grandfather.

Paul jumped up and ran to the refrigerator to get the salad started. While he was making the salad, he was thinking about the three weeks he spent with his friends every year during the month of July. He wished they lived closer together so they could see each other more often. Ariana lived in New Hampshire; Marisa in Colorado; and Samir's dad was a doctor in India. Samir's father taught at a local college during the summer months, and Samir always accompanied him to the United States.

During lunch, Grandfather asked Paul, "Do you think we can still call

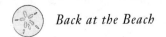

Ariana 'Curly Fries' this year? She had a birthday last month, and she's now eleven years old."

Paul smiled, and quickly responded, "Maybe not this year. She told me in an e-mail that her hair is really short now, and she has braces! I can't wait to see how she looks."

Grandfather handed a picture to Paul. "Here is a picture I took at the barbecue last summer of you and your friends. Maybe we can take another picture this year for our scrapbook," Grandfather said with a smile.

Paul looked at the picture and noticed how tall and slim Samir was even though he was always eating something! Samir said Indian food was very good and not

fattening. Marisa had a little red sailor's hat on top of her dark black hair, and her brown eyes were shining. Marisa and Ariana had their arms around each other in promise of being BFFs–best friends forever. Paul put the picture in his pocket to share with his friends.

When lunch was over, Paul unpacked his suitcase, carefully hanging up his clothes and lining up his shoes in the middle of the closet. When he was finished, he hugged his grandfather and started down the walkway towards the end of the road. He always enjoyed the smell from the sea breeze during the day and the magnificent sunsets in the evenings. In comparison to the plants growing in his yard in New Jersey, Paul noticed that most of the plants in Florida grew well in sand instead of dirt. Ms. Sarah's yard was quite unique because she did not have any plants, only sand, driftwood, and seashells, creating the illusion of an underwater garden above water! Paul took a few moments to study the shells. Once he began getting really hot in the sun, he opened the gate that led to Ms. Sarah's front porch. On the porch was a captain's bell for visitors to announce their arrival. Paul pulled the bell cord and listened to the distinct sound chiming through the house.

A quick burst of laughter broke out in the room inside the house and Ms. Sarah shouted through the screen door. "Paul Martin, come in, come in. Are you back for the summer?"

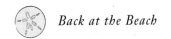

Paul opened the screen door and walked toward Ms. Sarah. "Yes, Ms. Sarah. I wanted to visit you today before my friends arrive."

Ms. Sarah said, "You look a lot taller. I'll bet you've grown at least two inches since last summer. How about some oatmeal cookies and pink lemonade for a growing boy."

Paul gave Ms. Sarah his finest smile and quickly replied, "Thank you Ms. Sarah. I would never turn down your homemade cookies and lemonade!"

Ms. Sarah brought the refreshments and Paul noticed she was moving very slowly. He suddenly remembered his grandfather mentioned Ms. Sarah was not feeling well. In a timid voice,

Paul asked, "Are you feeling okay Ms. Sarah?"

Ms. Sarah took a moment to sit down before slowly responding. "Yes, but I can't move as quickly as I used to."

Paul felt a little sad. "If there is anything I can do while I am visiting for the next few weeks, please let me know."

Ms. Sarah's face had a big smile as she replied, "I will, but for now I am just happy that you took the time to visit me today. Please remember that I always keep homemade cookies and lemonade in the kitchen for my special guests."

The lemonade was in front of them and as Paul munched on the cookies he told Ms. Sarah what he had done during the school year. He really enjoyed telling her about his extracurricular activity wrestling matches. At his school, a student had to maintain at least a "B" grade average in order to participate in after school activities.

At the end of the visit, Ms. Sarah said, "I saw you looking at the seashells in the front yard, and I would love to tell you about some of them the next time you come to visit."

"Thank you!" said Paul. "I will definitely come back and visit again, and if it is all right with you, I'll bring some friends with me."

As Paul got up to leave he noticed Ms. Sarah had some letters on the table by the front door, so he offered to carry them to the mailbox.

Ms. Sarah watched Paul going down

the steps with the letters in his hand and called out, "Thank you for visiting today and taking out the mail. I hope to see you and your friends real soon!"

THE SAND DOLLAR CLUB

The next morning after breakfast there was a knock at the door. After only a second, Samir opened the door and entered the room with a big smile.

"Hello, Paul. Hello, Mr. Brown. It is good to see everyone again. Can Paul come outside and play?"

Paul's grandfather smiled, his eyes full of light. "I don't mind if Paul goes

outside to play as long as his bed is made and his clothes are in order."

Paul and Samir ran out the back door, racing towards the beach and yelling to each other about what had happened during their last month in school. When they arrived at the beach it was deserted since it was still very early in the morning. Paul and Samir noticed the over-flowing garbage bins and the many seagulls that were starting to circle the bins.

"Guess the trash collection truck hasn't made it to this part of the beach yet," said Samir. "I wonder if we should try and put some of the overflow back into the garbage cans. We don't want the seagulls to try and pick at something that might hurt them."

"Great idea," said Paul. "And maybe we should get some huge garbage bags and collect the soda cans because I think we can cash them in for money at the recycling depot."

Samir nodded his agreement and Paul ran back to his grandfather's house to get the garbage bags. Samir started to pick up some garbage while Paul was gone and carefully put it back in the can while placing the aluminum cans on the side.

Paul returned after about five minutes with the plastic bag and two sets of gloves. "Grandfather is happy we are going to help keep the beach clean, and he will help us take all of the cans to the recycling depot just before we leave.

He wants us to wear gloves so we don't get cut with anything sharp and said we can store the bags of cans in the garage. Want to do this every morning?"

Samir smiled and replied, "Of course, maybe we will have a lot of money in two weeks, and then we can visit the water park!"

As they were carrying the bags filled with cans back to Paul's grandfather's house, they saw Ariana hanging out of her bedroom window and waving to them.

"I thought you were arriving later today," said Paul, "but I am very glad you are here now. Can you come out and play with us?"

Ariana began to laugh. She said, "I'll

be right out, and you definitely have to explain what you have in the garbage bags."

"Join us, and we'll tell you what is going on," he said. "We can definitely use another set of hands!"

Ariana joined the boys and heard about their idea to help keep the beach clean and earn money at the same time. Ariana was silent for a moment and then offered a suggestion. "Why don't we start a club since we have already established a project? We could set up some goals for the next few weeks and meet at seven every morning in front of the garbage bins."

"Sounds good to me," Paul said. Samir nodded in agreement.

"But we should think of a good name for the club," he said.

There was total silence for a few minutes while everyone was thinking really, really hard, and then Samir cried out. "How about the Sand Dollar Club since we always collect sand dollars to take home!"

Paul and Ariana agreed that "The Sand Dollar Club" would be a good name for their new club.

Ariana smiled a really big smile that showed her new braces and said, "We had better get to work because these bags have to be moved up the sidewalk and back to the garage."

"Do your braces hurt?" asked Samir with a frown on his face.

"No, and they don't come out unless I visit the dentist. I just have to brush my teeth as soon as I eat something."

Paul knew that Ariana was comfortable wearing her braces and asked, "How long will you have to wear the braces?"

"I have to wear them for one year, and I've already had them on my teeth for three months, so the time is passing quickly."

Paul laughed a little and in a low voice said, "I think you look very good with the braces."

Samir nodded in agreement and said, "I am getting very hot. I hope we can swim in the ocean when we are done with this project."

"What a wonderful idea!" said Ariana as she pulled her two bags.

"I agree," said Paul, and he continued up the sidewalk with his bags.

When the bags were neatly placed in the back of the garage, the group noticed it was starting to rain! All three club members gasped because they were really ready for a swim.

THE LEGEND
OF THE SAND DOLLAR

"What are we going to do?" said Ariana. "It's my first day at the beach; I don't want to play games in the house."

Paul smiled and said, "I have a great idea. Let's go visit Ms. Sarah at the end of the lane. She promised to tell us about some of the seashells in her yard if we

visit. We can ask her if it is all right to visit whenever it rains!"

Ariana, Paul, and Samir ran to Ms. Sarah's house and jumped up on the porch, each trying to ring the captain's bell first.

"Oh, this is my day," Ms. Sarah said. She quickly waved for the children to come into the house. "I like having special visitors, and I really enjoy talking about the treasures in my front yard."

Ariana ran over and gave Ms. Sarah a big hug, but she had a really puzzled look on her face. "What kind of treasures do you have in your yard? I only saw seashells and driftwood," she said.

Ms. Sarah, Paul, and Samir laughed loudly. Ms. Sarah said, "I consider the seashells to be my treasures, and you will understand why after I tell you about them. The seashells and driftwood was collected over the last forty years by family members walking along the beach. The sea holds many treasures, and there are forms of life that dwell on the beach or are cast up there. The sand on the beach is also filled with many living creatures in addition to these shells. We must always respect nature's treasures; after you look at a live shell, it should always be put back in the ocean.

Now it was time for Paul to look confused, and he asked, "Why do the shells have to be put back in the water after I look at them?"

Ms. Sarah's face had a big smile as

she responded to Paul. "That is a very good question young man. My family never collected live shells from the beach, only those shells that were empty after the snails had departed, or in the case of sponges, once it was no longer living. We must all do what we can to help preserve the environment. Does anyone have a favorite shell we should start with?"

The group cried out in unison, "Sand dollar please!"

Ariana quickly added, "Collecting sand dollars is something we all like to do so the sand dollar is our favorite seashell. We've decided to form a club since we all visit the beach together every year, and we named it "The Sand Dollar

Club." We want to have fun together and do something to help protect the environment. This year we are collecting aluminum cans to help keep the garbage cans on the beach from overflowing and keep the seagulls from getting hurt."

Ms. Sarah's eyes twinkled and she clapped her hands in approval because she believed that protecting the environment was a job for everyone. "The sand dollars, sometimes called sea biscuits, are flattened relatives of sea urchins. The size of the sand dollar is very different since the shells are flat and live in deeper water, where they are half half-buried in sand, feeding on organic material and plankton. When the sand dollar skeletons wash up on the beaches, they may be collected," said Ms. Sarah.

Paul said, "My family always chooses the best sand dollars, and we hang them on the Christmas tree with red ribbons."

Ariana said, "I always put some sand dollars in a basket in my room, and my mom has sand dollars in a basket on the outside patio!"

"Wow, my family puts sand dollars in a bowl with other shells, and some are on the patio as well. I also have some framed sand dollars hanging on the wall in my room!" said Samir.

Ms. Sarah expressed her delight at the many ways the children were using their sand dollars and asked Samir to help her carry the lemonade and cookies from the kitchen. Once they had the goodies in front of them, Ms. Sarah began reading from a piece of paper that she had taken out of her bible called "The Legend of the Sand Dollar."

There's a pretty little legend
That I would like to tell,
Of the birth and death of Jesus
Found in this lowly shell.

If you examine the sand dollar closely
You'll see that you find there
Four nail holes and a fifth one
Made by a Roman's spear.

On one side is the Easter Lilly
In the center is the star
That appeared unto the shepherds
And led them from afar.

The Christmas Poinsettia
Etched on the other side
Reminds us of his Birthday,
Our Happy Christmastide.

Now, break the center open
And here you will release
The five white doves awaiting
To spread good will and peace.

This simple little symbol
Christ left for you and me
To help us spread his Gospel
Through all eternity.

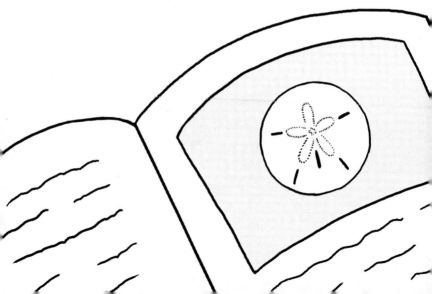

Ms. Sarah finished reading the legend, and the children were very quiet for several minutes thinking about the beautiful story of the sand dollar.

Samir broke the silence and had a very serious look on his face as he asked, "Ms. Sarah, should I put my sand dollar picture in the living room at Christmas time?"

Ms. Sarah gave him a big hug and said, "Of course, that is a very good idea, Samir."

Since it had stopped raining, Ms. Sarah asked the children if they wanted to learn how to clean seashells during their next visit.

"My shells always smell bad in the car during the trip home," said Ariana. "I would really like to know how to clean them properly."

Ms. Sarah smiled and said, "An official decision has been made by the members of the Sand Dollar Club. During your next visit, I'll explain how to clean and store seashells. Please bring some paper and a pencil to take notes."

As the children stood up to leave, Paul took a deep breath and said, "Is there anything we can do to help you Ms. Sarah? We are pretty good at taking out the garbage!"

Samir added, "If you need us for anything, just ring the captain's bell on the porch and we'll come running."

Ariana and Paul nodded in agreement, and then they all laughed.

Ms. Sarah stood up slowly and nodded her head to indicate she did not have anything for them to do, and then gave them each a big hug. "Thank you for coming. I am already looking forward to your next visit."

Since the rain had stopped the children ran down the sidewalk, making sure Ms. Sarah's gate was properly closed, and headed for the beach to gather seashells.

SEASHELL CLEANING

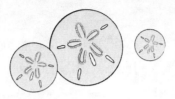

For the next two weeks, the children met every morning at seven to gather the aluminum cans and spent their days at the beach snorkeling and picking up seashells. On Sunday, it was raining so they quickly found Ms. Sarah after church and asked if they could visit her after lunch.

Ms. Sarah smiled and said, "That

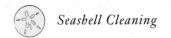

would be delightful. I had better get home and make some fresh cookies and lemonade."

After lunch Ariana, Paul, and Samir walked to Ms. Sarah's house, and they saw a girl on the porch swing at the house next to Ms. Sarah's.

"She has a cute pink hat–doesn't she remind you of someone?" asked Ariana.

"Marisa," said Paul and Samir in unison.

"Why don't we wave and see if she waves back?" said Ariana.

They all waived and Sofia left the porch and joined them at the front gate.

Ariana spoke first although they were all anxious to meet Sofia. "My name is

Ariana, and this is Paul and Samir," she said as she pointed to each of the boys. "We visit our grandparents every summer and have a lot of fun at the beach."

Samir joined in, "We have another friend whose name is Marisa, but she isn't here this year. We miss her and you remind of us of Marisa because she always wears a hat at the beach!"

After Paul was done laughing, he said, "Since it is starting to rain we are going to visit Ms. Sarah, who lives in the house next door. Would you like to join us?"

"I would love to go with you," said Sofia. "I just have to ask permission, if you can wait one minute. I am a very fast runner and will be right back."

Sofia returned quickly and the group walked to Ms. Sarah's house. It was decided Sofia could ring the bell since she was the newest member of the club.

When Ms. Sarah heard the bell she walked towards the screen door, but before she could open it, Ariana quickly said, "Hello, Ms. Sarah, this is Sofia our new friend, and I hope you will let her join us today."

Sofia waved her hand and with a big smile said, "Hi! I'm Sofia. May I please visit you today with Ariana, Paul, and Samir?"

Ms. Sarah opened the door and gave Sofia a big Ms. Sarah-style hug. "I would love to have another guest today, and there's enough cookies and lemonade for the entire neighborhood! Everyone should come in and take a seat. I'll go and get some paper and a pencil for Sofia to take notes, since I can see that everyone remembered to bring their notepaper and a pencil!" said Ms. Sarah.

When she returned, Ms. Sarah had a tray of cookies and lemonade for the children. After they were all nibbling on the cookies, Ms. Sarah explained that seashells with no animals inside are much easier to clean than seashells with live animal tissue. The outer covering of the shell should be cleaned by soaking the shell in a solution of half bleach and half water. The soaking time varies by the type of seashell and quantity of seashells being cleaned. The seashells should be checked every ten minutes, and removed from the solution when they are clean and white.

"*Always* wear plastic cleaning gloves and use tongs when placing or removing the shells in the bleach solution," said Ms. Sarah. "If after bleaching there are still some barnacles and other matter on the seashells, you can use an old toothbrush or grill brush to remove the remaining material. You may also use a file or sandpaper to smooth down chipped or rough parts of the shell if the natural state is not important. To shine your seashells, wipe them with mineral or baby oil. A helpful hint for transporting small sea-shells after they have been cleaned is to put them in egg cartons with cotton or tissue paper once they are dry. For larger shells, make sure the shell is nicely packed with cotton or tissue paper and not touching other shells."

Ms. Sarah asked, "Now that you have your notes, do you have any questions about the seashell cleaning process?" She took off her glasses, and looked closely at all four children. "No, Ms. Sarah," they responded in unison.

"We are going to have the cleanest shells in the country!" said Sofia.

"And we know how to get them home without breaking them," Paul added.

"My goodness, the sun is shining now," Ms. Sarah said. "You still have time to get to the beach today and find more shells!"

The children jumped up from the couch and carried all of the dishes to the kitchen. They gave Ms. Sarah a hug before they left.

"I am so glad to be visiting here this summer!" said Sofia. Ms. Sarah walked the children to the front door and continued waving until they were out of sight.

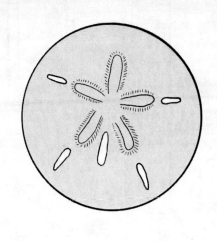
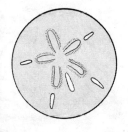
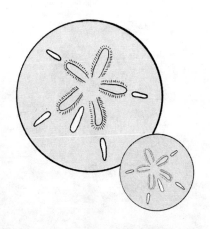

END OF SUMMER PARTY

Sofia joined the group for the next week, picking up cans and spending time with the members of the Sand Dollar Club. A few days before they were all due to depart, Paul asked his grandfather to drive them to the re-cycling depot to turn in the cans. Grandfather was more than happy to take the children to the recycling depot and they all rode in the back of the truck with the bags of cans and had a great adventure. There were so many cans, however, that two trips had to be made, and the total profit amounted to sixty-eight dollars. They now had more than enough money to pay for the water park tickets, so Paul called a meeting to plan the outing.

"I've never been to the water park," said Sofia. "What type of rides will we go on?"

Paul and Samir laughed, and Paul said, "There aren't any rides but the park has a lot of water activities like floating in tubes, sliding down into the water pools, and swiming with the plastic animals in the water."

Sofia was not as excited as the other

members of the Sand Dollar Club, so Paul asked her what she was thinking.

Sofia squirmed slightly in her chair and said, "Well, I have had the best time during my visit, especially after joining the Sand Dollar Club and spending time with Ms. Sarah. I am just wondering when we can all say good-bye to Ms. Sarah."

Paul's eyes blurred a little and he could feel his voice swelling in his throat. Everyone except Sofia had been caught up in the moment, and after a few moments he said, "I have a suggestion for the club to vote on–and if you agree we can skip the water park. I know you have all noticed that Ms. Sarah's glasses are taped together on both ends.

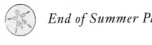

Why don't we buy new frames for her glasses with the money we made, and have a party at her house on the last day of Sofia's visit?

Sofia's hand flew up as she said, "As the newest member of The Sand Dollar Club, I vote yes!"

"I vote yes!" said Ariana.

"Samir said quietly with a mischievous smile, "Finally my turn. I agree!" and he clapped his hands loudly.

Paul said, "I'll ask grandfather to call Ms. Sarah's daughter and ask her to pick up Ms. Sarah's broken glasses when she takes her out this week. Her daughter doesn't live very far from the beach, but she has a job during the day or we could ask her to join the party. I know grandfather will help us get the eyeglass frames fixed, and we can give Ms. Sarah the repaired glasses at the party."

The children agreed the water park will still be there next year. Paul and the others told his grandfather what they planned to do and grandfather said he would call Ms. Sarah's daughter and arrange to have her get the glasses from Ms. Sarah. Paul said he would be responsible for calling Ms. Sarah to let her know the club members would be visiting on Friday to say goodbye.

At that point, Samir spoke up. "Mr. Brown, may we please bake cookies for Ms. Sarah at your house for the party? She always bakes cookies for us, and this time we can take cookies to her!"

"Excellent idea, Samir," commented Mr. Brown. "The Sand Dollar Club members can spend Friday morning in my kitchen baking cookies while I pick up the new glasses."

On Friday morning, there was a flurry of activity since the members of the Sand Dollar Club were busy at work in the kitchen making peanut butter cookies. When Mr. Brown returned with repaired glasses wrapped in beautiful paper, the children were ready to go to Ms. Sarah's house. They put the cookies on a platter covered with foil, and since it had been Paul's idea to get Ms. Sarah's glasses fixed, he was chosen to carry the package and Ariana carried the cookies.

Samir rang the captain's bell when they reached the house, and Ms. Sarah came to the door with a big smile on her face. "I am so glad you all took the time to come and say goodbye to me today," Ms. Sarah said.

"Please come in and sit down, and I'll get some cookies and lemonade for us."

Ms. Sarah had not noticed the tray of cookies in Ariana's hands since she was the last person through the screen door.

"We brought cookies and a gift for you!" Ariana said with a smile.

The club members gathered around Ms. Sarah while Samir volunteered to get the lemonade from the kitchen. After Samir returned, Paul passed out

the cookies they had made and handed Ms. Sarah her gift.

Ms. Sarah looked a little puzzled as she opened the package. When she saw her glasses with the new frames a little gasp of air escaped from her. "My goodness, what a blessing to have my eyeglass frames fixed, but where did you get the money to fix them?"

The children told Ms. Sarah about the Sand Dollar Club members' decision to spend the aluminum can money to fix her eyeglasses. Ms. Sarah was very quiet for a minute, and then she got up and gave them each a big hug!

After Ms. Sarah sat back down, Ariana finished a sip of her lemonade with a gurgling swallow and said, "Ms.

Sarah, you know we all love you and look forward to visiting you again next summer. But for the party today, *may we please have some of your cookies?* The cookies we made are not very good."

Everyone laughed as they followed Ms. Sarah to the kitchen to get her big tray of cookies!

e|LIVE

---

listen|imagine|view|experience